William Dunbar

Dunbar

Being a selection from the poems of an old makar

William Dunbar

Dunbar
Being a selection from the poems of an old makar

ISBN/EAN: 9783337206840

Printed in Europe, USA, Canada, Australia, Japan

Cover: Foto ©Andreas Hilbeck / pixelio.de

More available books at **www.hansebooks.com**

DUNBAR

BEING A SELECTION FROM THE POEMS OF
AN OLD MAKAR,
ADAPTED FOR MODERN READERS.

BY

HUGH HALIBURTON,

AUTHOR OF

"HORACE IN HOMESPUN," "OCHIL IDYLLS," ETC.

LONDON: WALTER SCOTT, LTD.,
PATERNOSTER SQUARE.
1895.

INSCRIBED TO

CHARLES ALFRED COOPER, Esq.,

WITH

EVERY SENTIMENT OF RESPECT

AND ESTEEM.

PREFACE.

TO WILLIAM DUNBAR.

From Scotland's later glory, Burns,
  The flower of Nature, fully blown,
My reverence instinctive turns
  To kneel at thy neglected throne,
Thou finer spirit, backward driven,
  Confined in priestly garments here,
Who found in Art a nearer heaven
  Wherein was neither sin nor fear.

With thee I tread the city ways,
  To wait at Royal James's court,
And watch with thine observant gaze
  Its pains, its follies, and its sport.
They welcome thee in bower and hall,
  The sprightly wits those chambers hold,
Thou alchemist, that turnest all
  In humour's crucible to gold.

Nor fails in thee the kindly heart
  That would thy brethren all embrace:
Beneath the friar's hood of Art
  Appears the thoughtful human face.
The mysteries of life and death
  Opprest thee, as they press us now;
Therefore is thine yet living breath—
  Our secret cares still speakest thou.

Thy fame, that waits in lingering bud,
  Had blossom'd long before our day,
But Flodden's red and raging flood
  Swept valour and thy voice away.
Alas, alas for Flodden yet,
  Heroic Scotland's early grave!
Can any after-growth forget
  The harvest sunk in Flodden's wave?

—OCHIL IDYLLS AND OTHER POEMS.

CHRONOLOGICAL TABLE,

ILLUSTRATIVE OF THE LIFE AND WRITINGS OF

WILLIAM DUNBAR.

1460. Probable date of his birth.

1475. Matriculation at St. Andrews University.

1477. Bachelor's degree.

1479. M.A. degree.

1480. About this time a novitiate (probably) in the Grey-friars' Convent, Edinburgh.

1491. A member of the Royal Commission in France.

1500. Pensioned, and in attendance at Holyrood.

1501-2. On an embassy to London.   Poet Laureate.

1503. Writes " The Thrissil and the Rose."

1508. Eight of his poems printed in Edinburgh by Chapman and Myllar.

1510. His pension raised to £80.

1513. In May, last notice of his pension. Battle of Flodden. Dunbar disappears from history.

1568. George Bannatyne collects fifty-one of Dunbar's poems. Sir Richard Maitland, about same time, collects twenty-seven.

1724. Allan Ramsay publishes in "The Evergreen" a large proportion of Dunbar's poems, copied from Bannatyne's MS., then in the possession of Sir James Foulis of Colinton House, Edinburgh.

1788. Discovery in Ayrshire of a unique copy of Chapman and Myllar's book of 1508. This was the first book that ever came from the Scottish Press. It is preserved (in its mutilated condition) in the Advocates' Library.

1834. First collected edition of Dunbar's Poems, by Dr. David Laing.

1883-93. Elaborate Edition, in Five Parts, by the Scottish Text Society; prepared by the late Dr. John Small, Professor Æneas Mackay, Rev. Dr. W. Gregor, and Mr. George P. M'Neill, LL.B.

CONTENTS.

———◆●◆———

		PAGE
SORROW ON HIMSEL'	. . .	11
THE USE OF RICHES	. . . .	13
CONTENTMENT	. . . . . .	16
THE TRUE PHILOSOPHY OF LIFE	. . .	19
HY-JINKS AT HOLYROOD	. . . .	22
TO THE P.D. DEMANDING COPY	. . .	26
THE PRIEST	. . . . . .	28
GNOMIC VERSES	. . . . . .	30
THIS WARLD'S VANITEE	. . . .	34
NOTHING SURE	. . . . .	37
PRAYER BEFORE THE SACRAMENT	. .	40
A MEDITATION IN WINTER	. . . .	42

	PAGE
THE VANITY O'T	45
EASTER HYMN	48
THE MAKAR'S COMPLAINT	51
A SONG OF RUE	54
THE GREATEST GAIN	56
TO MY LORDS OF 'CHACKER	58
ON CHANGE	60
JOHN TAMSON'S MAN	62
DISCRETION IN ASKING	64
CHANGE OF PARTY	67
REIGN OF COVETICE	69
THE THISTLE AND THE ROSE	72
DUNBAR'S DREAM	83
THE TWA CUMMERS	87
THE FRIARS OF BERWICK	89
DUNBAR FLYTING	103
A WELCOME TO THE LORD TREASURER	105
TO AN EDITOR	108
GLOSSARY	111

DUNBAR TO-DAY.

———•◆•———

SORROW ON HIMSEL'.

He that hes Gold and grit Richess.

THE man that siller has to spare,
  An' micht be happy late and ear',
    An' shivers in a hermit's cell,
Wi' hear'stane cauld an' basket bare—
    He brings his sorrow on himsel'.

The man that's free from care an' strife,
An' leads the single blessëd life,
    An' wi' the married state wad mell,
An' tak's in tow a thrawart wife—
    He brings his sorrow on himsel'.

He that wi' service fair an' true,
Wi' swink o' brain or sweat o' brow,
      Will in a house o' bondage dwell
Where merit never gat its due—
      He brings his sorrow on himsel'.

He that has treasure o' his ain,
A fair share o' this warld's gain,
      An' maun wi' foreign markets mell,
An' gets weel bitten for his pain—
      He brings his sorrow on himsel'.

He that may sit to cakes an' beer,
An' warm his virtue wi' gude cheer,
      An' ca's for water from the well,
An' suffers colic half the year—
      He brings his sorrow on himsel'.

Then, while we may, let us be merry,
An' care for no man's cant a cherry;
      But, while there is gude wine to sell,
Let him that on dry bread will worry
      Enjoy the drouth he gies himsel'.

THE USE OF RICHES.

Man, sen thy Lyfe is ay in Weir.

THERE are wha in this warld's strife
    O'erlook the terminus o' life
In trust o' what they ne'er attain,
Dissatisfied with every gain.

With toiling tired to bed they creep,
To toil they wauk again from sleep;
What profit hae they in their gain?
How can they ca' their gear their ain?

It's only theirs to haud thegither;
They only herd it for anither;
Death brings their tack o't to amane,
It's tint—and never was their ain.

In comes the heir, a graccless chiel,
A waif that never wuss'd them weel ;
He loups wi' glee, an' lauchs again—
I'se warrand that he mak's 't his ain !

Ithers there are like barren fools
Wha clock fu' cauld on cheeny bools,
An' streetch their wings, an' strive in vain
For chickens from a chucky-stane.

Wud to be rich, they want the pow'r ;
Their life is ae lang envious glow'r ;
Wi' glow'rin' at their neibour's gain,
They've tint conceit o' what's their ain.

Now ye that have achiev'd your share,
Wha hae to spend, an' think to spare,
I rede ye, owre an' owre again,
To tak' the use o' what's your ain.

It's no' just siller that mak's wealth :
There's love an' youth, an' hope an' health;
I rede ye therefore ance again
To tak' the use o' what's your ain.

CONTENTMENT.

Be mirry, man! and tak' nocht far in mynd.

B^E merry, friend! nor let it fret thy mind
    The wavering of this wretched warld of
        sorrow;
To Heaven be humble, to thy crony kind,
    And with thy neibours gladly lend and
        borrow:
    His chance to-night, it may be thine to-
        morrow;
Be blythe of heart whatever may befa',
    For, as wise men have said, an' proved afor-
        row,
Without content treasure is nocht ava.

Aye mak' the maist o' that which Fortune sends,—
  Then in adversity there's less annoy;
Nae gear is thine save only what thou spends,—
  The o'ercome's aften but a fashious joy.
  Let nae calamity thy strength destroy,—
For loss of heart is loss of life and a';
  But in fresh fields at once thy wits employ,
And find a shelter from the storms that blaw.

Live peaceably; flee quarrelling an' debate;
  Keep company with folks of honest fame;
Be frank and humble in a high estate,
  For Fortune's cheer is seldom lang the same.
  Spend not thy poverty in casting blame;
Be rich in patience, tho' thy gold's awa',—
  There's riches in a reputable name,
And, wanting that, treasure is nocht ava.

He's a puir scart wha sets himsel' wi' care
  To gather gear his sordid lifetime thro';
Wha, when his bags are fu', himself is bare,
  And of his riches but enjoys the view:

In comes anither, when the date is due,
A revelling youth that skails an' scatters a':
   Tak' thou the warning—or refuse an' rue
When owre thy een life's gloaming shadows fa'.

Tho' a' the wealth that ever was to wicht
   Fell in thy lap, not more thy share can be
Than meat, drink, claes, and o' the lave a sicht;
   An' yet keep mind thou maun a reckoning
      gie:
   It's easy richted when the reckoning's wee;
Be just an' joyous whether great or sma';
   An' keep this text before thine open ee—
Without content treasure is nocht ava.

THE TRUE PHILOSOPHY OF LIFE.

Full oft I muse and hes in thocht.

THE passage of the speeding year,
  And Fortune with her changing cheer,
    Are ills on ilka hand confest ;
We will not mourn for that, my dear,
    But to be blythe we'll count it best.

Fast as this warld fleets awa',
As fast her wheel does Fortune ca',
    At no time tired or takin' rest :
What then ? the limmer's owre us a',
    And to be blythe I think it best.

Would pamper'd man consider weel,
Ere Fortune on him turn her wheel,
      That earthly honour canna lest,
His fa' less painfu' he would feel :
      But to be blythe I think it best.

Wha would wi' this dour warld strive
Will a' his days in dolour drive,
      An', tho' he stood o' lands possest,
He couldna weel be said to live,
      He's only *tholin'* at the best.

Wi' a' the treasure i' the earth
What profit is there, wantin' mirth?
      Wi' a' the craps o' east an' west,
Without contentment there is dearth :
      So to be blythe is surely best.

Let nane for tinsel droop an' dee,
The thing is but a vanitee ;
      And to the life that aye shall lest
Here's out the twinkling of an ee :
      So to be blythe I think it best.

Had I, because my lot is puir,
Tint heart an' hope, an' harbour'd fear,
  An' been wi' carried cares opprest,
I had been dead langsyne I'm sure ;
  But to be blythe I think it best.

However Fortune change an' veer,
Let's blythely live as lang's we're here ;
  An' yet be ready and addrest
To pass content, without a tear,
  Believin' a' thing for the best.

HY-JINKS AT HOLYROOD.

Schir Jhon Sinclair begowthe to dance.

A PLEASANT nicht befel yestreen
　　In Holyrood the palace ;
A' kinds o' dancin' there was seen—
　　Except upon a gallace !
King Jamie crost his hunting legs,
　　An' sat into the lum,
An' drank a rouse to single jigs,
　　An' welcome a' that come
　　　　　　To loup that nicht.

And first Sir Andro, he maun prance,
　　An' he maun show his paces,
For he was new come oot o' France
　　Wi' a' the latest graces.

But as he caper'd fifty ways,
  An' bent his hochs, an' flang,
He burst the boddom o' his claes,
  An' darted thro' the thrang,
        An' hame that nicht !

Then stechy Tam, a forward fule,
  Wha never needit pressin',
Swore he would dance a *pas de seul*
  An' learn them a' a lesson.
But wae's me for the cratur's boast !
  For, wi' a kind o' stammer,
He loot an unexpected hoast
  That startled a' the chaumer,
        An' him that nicht !

Now wha cam next but Will Dunbar ?
  And nane cam' forrat franker,
For few within the land there war
  Sae souple-knee'd, or swanker.

He bobbit east, he bobbit wast,
   He turned upon a tae,
He trippit it fore-nenst his lass
   Until he cuist a shae
           Clean aff that nicht.

Then cam' the lass, a stately quean,
   Her very gang was gracefu';
Fra heels to head, and a' between,
   Her dancing charm'd the placefu'.
O when I saw her in the dance,
   Like Hebe loupin' fine,
I wuss'd I was the King o' France
   For *her* sake, and for mine,
           Loud out that nicht!

Neist cam' a carline up the flure
   That micht hae been a granny;
And nane was mair surpris'd, I'm sure,
   Than was her auld gudemanny.

Wi' gudewill to the wark she gade,
    But sune was sair forfoughen ;
An' wi' the awfu' mouths she made
    She set the king a-lauchin'
                A' owre that nicht !

Last in cam' Pate the porter tyke,
    Wi' ribbons at his knees ;
His feet were like a fa'in' dyke,
    His arms like flingin'-trees.
He stoiter'd like a hobbled mull
    The simmer clegs are gawin',
Till owre he whumml'd, length in full,
    An' fell'd Dunbar i' fa'in',
                An' a' the can'les !

TO THE P.D. DEMANDING COPY.

My Heid did yak sa yesternicht.

O MERCILESS are printers' bow'ls
To ane that in their service towls !
Their drudge he is baith nicht an' day—
Rewairdit when he looks for pay
Wi' twa-three groats an' twenty growls.

Wee deevil ! tell the maister-fien'
I had a toothache a' yestreen ;
And still sae sair in ilka jowl
The vermin stangs that, on my sowl,
I halflins wuss I hadna been !

I've fastit; an' I tried to pray;
I graned a' nicht—I girn the day:
  My wits I've sae completely tint—
  They're lyin' in my head ahint,
But whereawa' it's hard to say.

O wha can ply the rhymin' trade
Wi' a het toothache in his head?
  Or where's the fun that ithers see?
  Or what ambition can there be
To ane that's wussin' he was dead?

THE PRIEST.

Off Benefice, Schir, at everie Feist.

TO pick an' wale was for the priest;
 He aye was foremost at the feast,
  And to forbid him was to wrang him;
His crap was as the crap o' beast,
  And lay-folk only lived to pang him.

He flew at pheasant, flesh, an' fluke;
He made collusion wi' the cook
  For a' the choicest bits inside him;
But, lord! how piteous a' did look
  When to the haggis he applied him.

So wags this blind auld warld yet,
That to the greedy grants as debt
    What never did by richt belang them ;
While he that naething tak's can get
    Only a waiter's place amang them.

GNOMIC VERSES.

To Dwell in Court, my Friend, gife that thou
list.

MAXIMS of wisdom for ingenuous youth.
   First, envy nane ; content's the golden
      fee.
Listen an' look an' keep a steekit mouth ;
   The tongue that wags is no' the tongue that's
      free.
   Never retort on malice with a lee.
Forbear though friendship prompt, but most
      when pride,
   To counsel them that will not counsell'd be :
Ye do gey weel if weel yoursel' ye guide.

Wale weel your crony like a man o' sense ;
   He's no' aye leal that mak's a loyal show.
Risk not your fame in reckless confidence ;
   The flattering friend may prove the future
     foe.
In companies where thou art free to go
Be seen with men of mense, but turn aside
   From swicks and sweeps, the silly and the
     low :
The man does weel that sae himsel' can guide.

Have courage though nae lands can ca' ye
   laird ;
   Haud up your head—true manhood kens
     nae fear.
Ye have eneuch ? the rest may weel be spared ;
   Without content a millionaire is puir ;
   What pleasure has a miser wi' his gear?
What profit he that awns a warld wide
   Wi' death forenent him, drawin' near an'
     sure ?
Ye do gey weel if weel yoursel' ye guide.

Avoid the fellowship of men defamed.
　　Turn from the hollow tongue of flatterie.
Steer clear of slanderers; thou wilt be
　　blamed
　　For all the scandal of thy companie.
　　And stop the lug when envy tells the lee.
Leave wilful men with wilful men to chide;
　　What profit can it bring to them or thee?
Ye do richt weel if weel yoursel' ye guide.

And be not thou a whisperer in the nook;
　　Thae corner confidences folk suspec'.
Show scorn to nane, neither by lauch nor
　　look;
　　Into a noose the scorner rins his neck.
　　Be carefu' how ye counsel or correc'
Him that in counselling others tak's a
　　pride;
　　And first forecast the probable effec':
The man does weel wha weel himsel' can
　　guide.

And, since this life is full of ups an' downs,
  Stick to the ae thing certain—*Do what's
    due.*
The ne'er a thocht has Heaven o' coats an'
    gowns,
  Their fashion or their fabric, age or hue,
  But of the folk that fill them, me and you;
The warld's a stage, and this will a' decide
  When the play's owre—not *what* we
    play'd, but *hoo:*
And he plays best wha best himsel' can guide.

THIS WARLD'S VANITEE.

I that in heill wes and glaidnes.

HE stood on sic a stately shank
　　His health and happiness we drank,
And thocht for mony a year to see :
We little kenn'd this was to be.

The tass o' pleasure at his lip,
The strength o' manheid in his grip,
Ev'n as we gaz'd his vigour fail'd,
We scarce had time to say he ail'd.

Alas ! the line of human bliss,
How brittle and how brief it is !
How fast the silent Fury spins !
How swiftly to the reel it rins !

As willows in the wind that wave,
As grasses trembling on a grave,
So fluctuates in th' unequal strife
The passive chance of human life.

What stay endures? What state stands
  fast?
What shelter can secure at last?
What charm avert, what skill withstand
That fateful, strong, forth-reaching hand?

It parts the monarch and his pride;
It tak's her bridegroom from the bride;
The infant sleeping on her sleeve
It lifts without the mither's leave.

The warrior from the battle's din;
The traveller tarrying at the inn;
The bairnie playing wi' his ba';—
It tak's them ane, it tak's them a'.

Even the doctor, fat wi' fees,
An' letter'd thick wi' learn'd degrees,
It tak's him from his patient's bed,
It tak's him in the patient's stead.

Lawyers ana, a jinkin' band,
Maun tak' their summons from that hand ;
An' makars too, wi' catchin' breath,
Maun stap aside to speak wi' Death !

Since a' that ever lived are gane,
Since we but tarry till we're ta'en,
Best is that we for Death prepare
By taking in this warld wir share.

NOTHING SURE.

Quhome to sall I complene my wo.

TO whom shall I complain my wo?
　　To whom shall I for counsel go?
I know not, amang rich or poor,
Who is my friend, who is my foe;
　　For in this warld there's naething sure.

To whom shall I go make my moan?
For service lang, rewaird is none;
　　And short my life may now endure;
And lost is a' the time by-gone;
　　And in this warld there's naething sure.

Here mockery rides with hand on rein ;
While merit pads it on the plain,
 Sweats in the sun, an' bides the stour ;
I've seen it owre an' owre again—
 Within this warld there's naething sure.

Here Flattery wears a purfled goun,
And Falsehood with a lord sits doun,
 While Truth is hounded from the door,
And Honour banish'd from the toun :
 Within this warld there's naething sure.

Where lives the man so cased in plate
That he can stand the stroke of fate ?
 Or where is he whose glance secure
Can spy the wo that lies in wait ?
 Within this warld there's naething sure.

Fair word from every mouth proceeds,
In every heart deception breeds ;
 From every ee goes look demure,
But from the hand go few good deeds :
 Within this warld there's naething sure.

Lord ! since in time, so soon to come,
De terra surrecturus sum,
    What needs I care for earthly cure ?
Tu regni da imperium,
    For here at least there's naething sure.

PRAYER BEFORE THE SACRAMENT.

I Cry the Mercy and Lasar to Repent.

TO Thee, to Thee alone, Redeemer mine,
   My King, my Friend, my gracious Saviour
     sweet,
Before Thy bleeding body I incline,
   And for my sins forgiveness thus entreat,
   That ever I did, up to this hour complete,
In act, or word, or unexprest intent;
   Down on my knees, fu' low before Thy feet,
I mercy beg, and leisure to repent.

Lord, I confess that I neglected have
   Sweet Mercy's code, in spirit and in letter;
Nor meat nor money to the sterving gave;
   Nor saw the sick, nor socht to mak' them
     better:

Nor clad the naked; nor relieved the debtor;
Nor of puir waifs an' wayfarers took tent;
    And would have pass'd the Magdalen had I
        met her:
I mercy beg, and leisure to repent.

Thy wise commands—to honour Thee alone;
    Nor tak' Thy name in vain; nor thief to be;
To covet no man's aucht, pleased with my own;
    Falsehood to shun, an' youthfu' lusts to flee;
    To act obedient to a parent's ee;
To follow none with murderous intent:
    Lord, for a broken law I lout to Thee,
And mercy beg, and leisure to repent.

Though I have not Thy precious feet to kiss,
    As Magdalen had when she did mercy crave,
I'll weep like her for all I've done amiss,
    And every morning seek Thee at Thy grave:
    Therefore forgive me as Thou her forgave;
Thou know'st my heart, like hers, is penitent;
    And grant, ere I the sacrament receive,
Pardon, and love, and leisure to repent.

A MEDITATION IN WINTER.

In to thir dirk and drublie Dayis.

IN Winter's dull an' drumlie day,
   When Nature dons her dark array,
   An' the lang tempest howling flies,
   Mingling in ruin earth an' skies,
Sma' heart hae I to sing or play.

But maist when nicht draws out the hours
Wi' wind an' hail an' heavy show'rs,
   My spirit sinks as in a tomb
   For lack o' Simmer and her bloom
And a' the beauty of her bow'rs.

I toss, I turn; sleep can I nane;
Doubt an' dark fears disturb my brain:
   This warld a' owre I cast about
   For something to dispel my doubt,
But cast about this warld in vain.

Despair is ever at my side,
" Provide!" he cries; "in time provide:
   Ye've wair'd or wastit a' your prime;
   Now think upon your latter time—
How will ye live? whaur will ye bide?"

Then Patience, counselling hope an' faith,
" Hold fast," she cries, " thy grip o' baith!
   Fortune's a jade—but cease to murn,
   Her wheel erelang will tak' a turn;
She'll mind ye yet, I'se tak' my aith!"

Then Wisdom, as I glance her way,—
" Why fash to get what cannot stay,
   Or can be thine but little space,
   Thou tending to another place,
A journey going every day?"

And then says Age—"My friend, come near;
Why shouldst thou start when I appear?
　　Come, brother, by the hand me tak':
　　Remember thou has count to mak'
Of a' the time thou spendest here."

Syne Ane, a low door opening wide,
Says—"I am Death; and here I bide,
　　And never yet was man sae stout
　　But to this lintel he maun lout:
There is nae ither way beside!"

Wi' fear o' this a' day I droop;
Nae coin in kist, nae wine in cup,
　　Nor woman's grace, nor loving kiss
　　Can keep me from remembering this,
How blythe soe'er I dine or sup.

Yet when the nichts begin to short,
It cheers my spirit in a sort,
　　Care-darken'd wi' the winter show'rs.
　　Come, loesome Simmer! wi' thy flow'rs,
That I may live in some disport.

THE VANITY O'T.

All erdly Joy returnis in pane.

LATE as ae winter's nicht I lay
  An' wearied for the licht o' day,
My thochts ran in a waefu' train
That a' this warld was made in vain.

Richt weel we ken that fail we must;
The strongest body is but dust,
And shall to dust return again :
Surely the strength of man is vain.

We see that auld age swallows youth—
If it escape that gaping mouth
That tak's baith rick an' ripening grain :
Surely the flower of youth is vain.

Siller an' silks an' saft array—
What are they if they lie our way
But thorns wi' flow'rs an' leaves o'erlain ?
Surely this warld's wealth is vain.

Cam' never budding hope sae green
But disappointment cam' as keen ;
We trust, but never do attain :
Surely the hopes of man are vain.

Oh, wha can doubt that after joy
There's ever something to annoy ?
Now, since they canna aye remain,
Surely the joys of life are vain.

Friendship an' love are fair an' sweet,
Friendship an' love are aft deceit ;
The words are fause that mak' us fain :
Surely the loves of man are vain.

How aft the kindest heart that is
Grows cauld an' hard in avarice !
How aft wi' greed is conscience slain !
Surely our virtues are in vain.

Yet since 'tis fate that rules it a',
And life's short day slips fast awa',
Let's tak' the pleasure wi' the pain—
It has its value though it's vain.

EASTER HYMN.

Done is a Battell on the Dragon Blak.

THE fight is ended with the dragon black,
    Christ stands victorious in the deadly stour,
The gates of hell are broken with a crack,
    High shines the cross in this triumphant
        hour ;
    See in the shade where devils trembling cow'r,
While ransom'd souls to blissful freedom go
    Singing aloud their mighty champion's pow'r—
Surrexit Dominus de sepulchro.

Scotch'd is the laidly dragon Lucifar,
    The cruel serpent with the mortal stang,
The auld keen tiger with his teeth ajar
    That had in ambush lain for us sae lang,

Thinking to grip us in his talons strang ;
Thanks to our Lord that would not have it so,
But flew and snatch'd us from his pointed
fang—
Surrexit Dominus de sepulchro.

He for our sake that was a babe and slain,
And like a lamb in sacrifice was dight,
Is like a lion risen up again,
Or like a man with a great giant's might.
Fled is the darkness in disorder'd flight,
And yonder shines the glorious morning-glow,
Eternal day dawns on the dreary night—
Surrexit Dominus de sepulchro.

Our vicar from the grave is risen again
That in our quarrel to the death was wounded;
The sun that shrank in gloom now shines
amain ;
Darkness removed, our faith is now re-founded;

The bells of mercy from the heavens have
  sounded;
The christians are deliver'd from their wo
  And of their crime the Jews now stand con-
  founded—
Surrexit Dominus de sepulchro.

The foe in flight, the struggle now may cease;
  The tolbooth's broken and the dungeon
  tumed;
The war is owre, establish'd is the peace;
  Lowsed are the fetters and the jailers lamed;
  The ransom paid, the prisoners are redeemed;
All's done—all's won! baith spulzied is the foe
  And plunder'd o' the spulzie that he claimed—
Surrexit Dominus de sepulchro.

THE MAKAR'S COMPLAINT.

Faine wald I with all Diligence.

FAIN would I mak' a noble sang
  That should thro' a' the kintra gang
   An' fill the lug o' Scotland quite ;
The luck to Lewis may belang—
  I ken it's no' in me to write.

For tho' I waited seven lang year,
An' plann'd the wark, an' made it clear,
  An' soberly sat doun to 'dite,—
Hunders there are would snarling speir
  Gif I had been advis'd to write.

And first my maitter they would blame,
And, tho' I never mention'd name,
      Would put upon my head the wite
Of blackening their honest fame;
      And thus I kenna what to write.

If in my sang I prais'd a deed
Dune by a bairn of noble breed,
      Then would they say I flatter'd quite,
Finding my motive in their greed;
      And thus again it's hard to write.

But if mean actions I decry—
O waur than flatterer then am I,
      I live to slander an' backbite:
Nae wonder at this warld I sigh
      And say I kenna what to write.

Unless I mak' to this man's mind,
Howe'er its bias is inclin'd,
      My makin', sir, 's no' worth a mite;
But critics are a contrar' kind,
      An' wha to please them a' can write?

But when they a' begin to bowff
Till misery haunts the muse's howff,
     Better I left the paper white
An' took to poaching, or to gowff,
     Than write an' kenna what to write.

A SONG OF RUE.

Sweit roiss of vertew and of gentilnes.

THY glance, thy grace, thy winsome face,
  And a' the charms about thee, O,—
O woman fair! what man could dare
  To look an' live without thee, O?
But oh! the pity of it, sweet!
   Though fair thou art,
   Thou hast no pity in thy heart
To mak' thy charms complete!

Thy beauties a', sae fair they shaw,
  To me they're like a garden, O;
Thrice happy he that has the key,
  He's mair than king that's warden, O.

But in this garden fair to view,
    Where lilies fine
    With roses red and white combine,
I miss the plant o' rue!

I fear the norlan' winds hae blawn,
    An', though they've spared a hantle, O,
The sweetest seed that e'er was sawn—
    They've killed the braird sae gentle, O!
It gie's my heart sae sair a pain
    That I maun greet,
    Amang sae mony flow'rs sae sweet,
Until it grows again!

THE GREATEST GAIN.

Quho thinkis that he has sufficience.

HE'S no' to maen, he needna murn
    Wha has enow to serve his turn;
And he that has baith stock an' rent
May fling his siller down the burn—
    It's naething if he's no' content.

Therefore, although, my brither dear,
Few dainties at thy board appear,
    Say grace to God for what is sent,
And of it gladly mak' gude cheer:
    He has enow that is content.

If thou hast riches, deal them free ;
And if thou stand in povertee,
    To stand in povertee consent ;
There's weal that wealth can never gie ;
    And he's providit that's content.

Lastly, my friends an' brethren a',
If in this life ye've lairdship sma',
    The less your fasherie thereanent :
He that is low can hardly fa',
    And he has plenty that's content.

TO MY LORDS OF 'CHACKER.

My Lordis of Chacker, pleis yow to heir.

YE clerks that owre the cash preside,
  Weel may ye wear a sleekit hide,
  And weel may hardihood be yours !
  Ye little ken what he endures
Wha hasna siller at his side.

Nae doot ye wonder why I'm here :
Listen, and I shall mak' it clear
    As simmer when the days are fine ;
    For left is neither cross nor coin
Of a' my income for the year.

To reckon up my rents an' roums
I dinna need to tire my thoums,
    Nor yet to gar my counters clink,
    Nor paper to expend, nor ink,
In the receipting o' my soums.

I gat from that chield sitting there,
Some sax months syne, my annual share :
    I canna tell ye how it's spendit
    But weel I wat the siller's endit ;
An' what's the use o' reckoning mair ?

I mind I trow'd, what time I took it,
It would be lang ere I was rookit :
    Miscalculation's been my curse ;
    I hae nae proof o't but my purse,
Which wouldna lee gin it were lookit.

Sae, no' to keep ye idle mair,
Disburse what moneys ye can spare,
    Report it to the next account,—
    It can but lessen the amount ;
And may your baskets ne'er be bare !

ON CHANGE.

I seik abowte this warld onstable.

SAE cockerty it is, an' cantit,
    Weel micht this warld be supplantit
        By something steadier than is ;
        For what o't can ye say but this,
That naething happens as ye want it?

But yesterday the sun shone fair,
Blue was the sky, balmy the air,—
        The warld was like a peacock feather :
        The day—it's stinging like a nether,
And boisterous as a wauken'd bear.

But yesterday, fair sprang the flow'rs;
The day—they're slain wi' sleety show'rs;
    An' bees that bumm'd, an' birds that sang,
    Till Simmer wi' their service rang,
Are shivering in their bykes an' bow'rs.

Thus Winter comes at Simmer's e'en;
Thus after comfort care blaws keen;
    And tho' from midnight comes the
      morrow,
    As certainly from joy comes sorrow:
Such is this life, and aye has been.

JOHN TAMSON'S MAN.

Schir, for your Grace bayth Nicht and Day.

SIR, on my knees, baith nicht an' day,
    Sincerely from my soul I pray,
Wi' a' the fervour that I can,—
Oh that ye were John Tamson's man!

For, were it sae, then weel were me;
Without a place I wouldna be;
Endit were my misfortunes than,
If ye were ance John Tamson's man.

My advocat', baith fair an' sweet,
(Lang has she been, lang maun she be't!)
Would speed in my puir errand than,
If ye were but John Tamson's man.

What hurt were dune, what harm could be,
Tho' ane, sae fair an' sweet as she,
Such influence owre your dourness wan
As to mak' you John Tamson's man ?

Does that affection stand the test
That's mated wi' the first an' best
In Britain since the warld began
An' fears to be John Tamson's man ?

Thrissle ! we ance did a' suppose
The mercy o' the sweet meek rose
Would mould ye to a milder plan
By makin' ye John Tamson's man.

POSTSCRIPT.

I find him deaf I fand sae dour,
Sae pitiless to me sae poor;
I can but end as I began—
I wuss he was John Tamson's man !

DISCRETION IN ASKING.

Off every asking followis nocht.

REMEMBER, when ye ask for ocht,
　　Let it be seasonably socht,
An' when there's reason folk will see;
An' when there's nane it will be thocht
　　Discretion should in asking be.

The man's a fule that, reason or nane,
Eternal seeks in ceaseless rane;
　　Aye harping in a carping key,
He gets a hearer dull as stane:
　　Discretion should in asking be.

Some ask for mair than they deserve;
Some ask for naething—and they sterve;
  Others again, shamefac'd like me,
In ill-rewairdit silence serve:
  Discretion should in asking be.

To beg will hurt an honest name;
To crave your ain, you're no' to blame;
  To serve, an' live in beggaree,
To man an' maister baith's a shame:
  Discretion should in asking be.

He that has wrocht, an' dune his best,
Needs not to mak' it manifest
  Wi' mony words to them that see;
Few words gang to a wise request:
  Discretion should in asking be.

It will not answer to be dumb,
For naething of itsel' will come:
  Then wale your wordies, twa or three,—
Whatever's got is got wi' some:
  Discretion should in asking be.

5

Some micht have Ay! an' higher place,
That get a naysay to their face
    For want of a discerning ee;
They tyne their errand in disgrace:
    Discretion should in asking be.

Tho' service may gang lang unquit,
Rewaird at last we'll surely get;
    If not—alas! what remedie?
To fecht wi' fate shaws little wit;
    We'll ask discreetly,—and we'll dee.

CHANGE OF PARTY.

Schir, at this Feist of Benefyce.

NOW that appointments are to mak',
And mony hands are stretch'd to tak',
Sir, I mak' bauld advice to gie ;—
Better a place,
Tho' but within the door it be,
Than let a loyal servant lack
For faut o' grace.

For whether is the merit mair
To gie him drink that's thirsting sair,
Or fill a fu' man till he burst—
Leaving to pine
His fallow perishing o' thirst,
Wha maybe mair deserving were
To swallow wine.

It's hardly a convivial toun
Where Jock looks merry an' John looks doun,
    Where Watty swallows like a trout
        An' Davy's dry;
    . Na! let the caup gang round about
From lip of lord to lip of loon—
        Fairplay! say I.

THE REIGN OF COVETICE.

Ffredome, Honour and Nobilnes.

IT was a happier warld in sooth
   As I remember't in my youth:
We're aff upon a new device,
We're a' gaun wrang thro' covetice.

O gie me back the by-gane days,
The big, free-handit, hearty ways!
Ye're a' sae nippit an' sae nice,
Ye're a' gane wrang thro' covetice.

Whaur are the social lives we led,
Whaur are the social games we hed?
There's nae play noo but cards an' dice,
The warld's changed thro' covetice.

O mony a laird in mony a toun
'S a near-be-gaun an' niggart loon
Whase faithers never kent the vice,
And a' thro' cause o' covetice.

In brughs to landwart an' to sea,
Where peace an' plenty wont to be,
Pleasure's gane up to famine price,
And a' thro' faut o' covetice.

Farmers that hed a saddle seat,
Wi' kye an' corn to sell an' eat,
Keep nae beast noo but cats an' mice,
And a' thro' cause o' covetice.

He that to friendly deeds inclin'd
Would live at peace wi' a' mankind,
He's lauch'd at for his simple ch'ice,
And a' thro' cause o' covetice.

But he that aff his neighbour man
Rives a' the profit that he can,
He's ca'd an active chield, an' wice,
And a' thro' cause o' covetice.

Man, please thy Maker an' be merry,
And set not by this warld a cherry,
Work for the place of paradice
For therein reigns nae covetice.

THE THISTLE AND THE ROSE.

Quhen Merche was with variand Windis past.

WHEN Merch with his unruly winds was
  past,
 And April, that cam' in with peevish show'rs,
Had like a tinkler tane her leave at last,
 And May, that should be mither to the
  flow'rs,
 Had choused the birds back to the frozen
  bow'rs
Amang the orchards, reddening in despite,
Whose sangs to hear it was a sad delight;

In bed one morning as I dovering lay,
 Methought Aurora with her glimmering een
Stole to my lattice at the dawn of day,

And looking in with visage pale and green
Invited me to rise and write the scene
With " Waken, poet ! from your slumbering,"
And " Listen to the linties how they sing."

And then methought before my bed upstood
    Fair May herself in habit rich and new,
With such a pleasant face as did me good,
    And such a posy bright with blabs o' dew
    And gay with colour, red and white and blue,
That it both filled and overflowed my dream,
And all the house enlivened with the gleam.

" Poet ! " she said, "my poet ! rise for shame,
    And in my honour take thy pen and write ;
Hear how the larks the merry day proclaim
    To waken lovers to their own delight.
    Once thou wert fain and foremost to indite,
Thy heart—time was—has glad and blissful
        been,
Making for me under the leaves sac green."

"Wherefore should I uprise at early morn?
    At this cauld season wha (said I) can sing?
Mair cause hae I to weep and wail forlorn,
    May days that were of old remembering:
    May days they were—but these are no such
        thing.
Rise they wha like to thole your sleety scorn,
Amang your bow'rs to walk I have forborne."

Thereat the lady placidly did smile,
    And said, "Uprise and 'sey thy wonted
        pow'rs;
Hast thou forgot thy promise made erewhile
    To celebrate in May the queen of flow'rs?
    Lo! here is May: the birds are in their
        bow'rs,
The sun is shining on their feathers bright,
And song is welling from their bosoms light."

She turned and went, and with her all the gleam
    That such a glory to my chamber lent;
At which, methought, for it was still a dream,

In sark and mantle after her I went
Into a garden, fair and full of scent,
With herbs, and plants, and paths for naked
    feet,
Fragrant of breath and fresh with morning's
    weet.

Just then the sun on wings of orient red
    Did as an angel in the east appear ;
A twist of gold enclosed his shapely head,
    And his long tresses glittered golden clear ;
    And all the world beholding, far and near,
Took comfort looking on his blissful face,
And blessed him with his own reflected grace.

And him the only ruler of the sky
    The cock did first proclaim with martial
        might,
And next with choral throats the birds did cry
    " Begone, thou foe to love ! away, dull night !
    But welcome, day ! that comforts every
        wight ;

And welcome May-time, flow'rs, and morning
    sheen,
And nature's charms, and love—of all the
    queen."

Dame Nature then gave inhibition there
    To Neptune fierce and Æolus the bauld
Not to perturb the water nor the air,
    And that no show'r of hail nor snip of cauld
    Should do offence to flow'r in field or fauld;
And Juno too she bade, that bides on high,
To keep it fine, and fair aboon, and dry.

She next ordained that every bird and beast
    Before her presence should at once appear,
And every bloom of virtue, most and least,
    And herb of field or forest, far and near,
    As they were wont in May from year to
        year:
She was their maker, and it bude them a'
To own her orders and respect her law.

With that she straight dispatched the souple roe
    To gather in the beasts of every kind;
The swallow she deputed next to go
    And fetch the birds, leave none of them
        behind;
    And for the flow'rs she thought within her
        mind
There was the gowan—but she sent the yarrow,
And forth it sprang as fleet as flying arrow.

Then swith, within the twinkling of an ee,
    Beast, bird, and flow'r were a' before their
        queen;
And first the lion, foremost in degree,
    Was summoned forward: with respectful mien,
    But with a hardy countenance and keen,
Before the Dame he cam' and bowed the knee—
Yet nane the less a lion bauld was he.

This is the creature that gars others quake;
    Strong-faced and stern he is, of piercing ee,
Unmatchable in grace and strength of make,

Well-knit, and in his motions light and free.
Red is the ruby, and like that is he;
Ramping in field of gold he standeth stout,
With fleur-de-luces circled all about.

The lady stooped and lifted up his paw,
    And kindly let him lean upon her knee,
And crowned him with a diadem sae braw,
    Blazing with gems it was a joy to see;
    "And now thou art the King of Beasts," said
        she,
"And lord protector of the woods and shaws,
Go to thy lieges and uphold the laws.

Be just at first and merciful at length;
    And let no wee beast suffer scaith nor scorn
From bigger beast that would misuse its
        strength;
    Do law alike to ape and unicorn;
    And let nae bull with an aggressive horn
The meek plough ox oppress in sulky pride,
But in the yoke draw doucely him beside."

And next she crowned the eagle King of Fowls,
   And gave him vision far and speed of pens;
And bade him be as fair to whaups and owls
   As unto peacocks, popinjays, and crenns;
   And mak' ae law for craws and kittie-wrens;
And let no bird of ravenous beak affray
Nor massacre except for lawful prey.

Then summoned she the flow'rs; the flow'rs
   obeyed;
   This with its bud, that with its bell appears;
At last her look upon the thistle stayed,
   She saw him kepit with a bush of spears,
   She found him apt and able for the weirs,
So him she crowned, red was the crown she
   gave,
And said "In field go forth and 'fend the lave.

And since thou hast the crown be thou discreet,
   And give each plant its proper rate and
      price,
For some are virtueless, and some are sweet,

And some are like the nettle full of vice;
  You would not match it with the fleur-de-lys;
The lily to the weebie must not yield,
You would not let it drive her from the field.

And hold no other flow'r in equal fame
  With the fresh rose, the rose both red and
    white,
For if thou do thy judgment is to blame,
  For there is none though fair to match her
    quite,
  So sweet of breath, so pleasant to the sight,
So graceful or so gracious none can be,
So worth thy worship every way as she."

Then on the rose she turned a gracious glance,
  And said "O loveliest daughter of the Spring,
Lift up with joy thy blushing countenance
  And in thy praise shall grove and garden ring;
  Thou needs but look to have a welcoming.
Come, bloom of bliss, and wear the diademe,
For owre the lave thy beauty shines supreme."

Then with a crown with many a jewel bright
  Nature methought did her fair brows en-
    close
And all the land illumined with its light;
  Whereat a cry from all the garden rose
  Of "Welcome, that art the fairest flow'r that
    blows!
Welcome, that worthy art to be our queen!
That to be honoured needs but to be seen!"

It was the saft voice of the flow'rs I heard:
  And then the birds methought took up the
    tune;
And first it was a solitary bird,
  The mavis first, and then the merle, and
    soon
  The nightingale below, the lark aboon;
And "Hail," they sang, "the rose both red and
    white!"
And "Hail," they sang, "the rose of most
    delight!"

6

Then all the birds burst forth with sic a shout
   I started in my sleep, and woke anon,
But missing all the pleasance turned about
   To dream again : alas ! the dream was gone.
   Then up I rose, and wandered forth alone,
And mused, and made what ye have heard me
     say,
On the ninth morning of the present May.

DUNBAR'S DREAM.

This hinder Nycht befoir the dawing cleir.

L AST nicht, some time before the dawing
    clear,
Methocht Saint Francis did to me appear
    With a religious habit in his hand,
      And said, "In this go cleed thee, William,
      and
Gie up the warld, for thou maun be a freer."

Wi' him an' wi' his habit I was scaur'd,
Suner a ghaist i' gloamin' I wad daur'd,
    But when i' bed he laid it me abune,
      Upon the flure richt cleverly an' sune
I lowpit out, an' never wad come nar'd.

Quo' he, " What ails thee at the haly weed?
Cleed thee therein, for wear it thou must need :
     Thou that has lang made sangs for all and
         each,
     Sall now be freer, and in this habit preach;
Mak' no delay—it maun be done indeed."

Quo' I, " Saint Francis, loving be thee till,
An' thankit mote thou be for thy gudewill
     In being wi' thir claes to me sae kind ;
     But then (quo' I) they're hardly to my
         mind ;
If I refuse them, dinna tak' it ill.

Of legends of the saints I've read eleven,
An' there I find the bishops number seven ;
     The rest were freers, an' few they were
         indeed ;
     Therefore gae bring to me a bishop's weed
If ever thou would my soul should come to
         heaven."

"Ye ken," quo' then Saint Francis, losing
        patience,
" The brethren oft have made thee supplications
        To tak' the habit, but thou did postpone ;
        But ony mair ado, therefore, come on,
An' mak' nae langer silly excusations."

Quo' I, " But I was ance a prentice freer ;
The date thereof is past fu' mony a year,
        But a' thro' England, southward to Calace,
        In every burrowstoun an' country-place,
Drest in that habit have I made gude cheer.

In it I've bann'd an' beggit, lee'd an' fleech'd ;
In it in every pu'pit have I preach'd
        South from Corstorphine Kirk to Canter-
        bury ;
        In it I past at Dover owre the ferry
To Picardy, an' there the people teach'd.

As lang as I did bear the freer's style,
My life, gude kens, was ae lang wicked wile :
  In me was inclination aye to flatter,
  And, what will wash out wi' nae haly watter,
I was aye ready a' men to beguile."

The freer that did Saint Francis there appear—
The fiend he was, in likeness of a freer!
  Wi' horns aneath his hood! And as I spoke
  He vanish'd in a flash o' fire an' smoke,
Vanish'd, an' took the house-end wi' him near!

THE TWA CUMMERS.

Rycht airlie on Ask Weddinsday.

RICHT early on Ash-Wednesday
  Drinkin' the wine sat cummers tway;
The tane did to the tither complain,
Sichin' an' sowpin' did she say—
  This lang Lentern mak's me lean.

On stool beside the fire she sat;
Gude kens if she was grit an' fat;
  Yet to be feeble she did feign,
And aye she said " Here's proof o' that;
  It's the lang Lentern mak's me lean."

"My fair sweet cummer," quo' the tither,
"Ye tak' your leanness aff your mither;
   A' kind o' wine she would disdain
But malvaisie—she'd bide nae ither."
   This lang Lentern mak's me lean.

"Cummer, be blythe, baith e'en an' morrow,
An' let your husband drie the sorrow;
   But you from fasting should refrain;
And I'se uphaud, St. Bride to borrow,
   That Lentern shall not mak' you lean."

"Your counsel, cummer, 's gude," quo' she;
"Fill a fu' caup, an' drink to me;
   That man o' mine's no' worth a bean:
This is the only joy I ha'e,
   And Lentern shall not mak' me lean."

Thir twa, out of a mutchkin stoup,
They drank twa chappin, sowp for sowp,
   Sae great a drouth did them constrain;
By then to mend they had gude howp
   And Lentern wouldna mak' them lean.

FRIARS OF BERWICK.

As it Befell and happinit into deid.

DOWN at the mouth o' Tweed there stands
　　a toun
Wi' tours o' strength an' stane wa's girdled roun',
And a great castle seen far aff at sea,
A lastin' landmark in the sailor's ee.

But to tell owre its strength an' warlike stores,
Its ports an' pends, hinged brigs an' slidin'
　　doors,
Merlons aloft, wi' morions glancin' clear,
Hackbuts, an' scaldin' pats, an' siclike gear,
Crossbows, an' cracks, and other gins o' death,
Shot-holes a' doun, an' double stanks beneath—

The bare account would need a lang day haill,
An' nae ways help the progress o' my tale.

The toun was thus, as ye may weel suppose,
Safe for its friends an' prief against its foes;
An' meikle was the need o' bar an' gin,
For meikle was the merchandise therein.

Ships from a' shores met in the river's mouth,
An' mixed the treasures o' the north an' south;
But at the ports what chafferin' was to hear!
And on the streets, what thrang o' folk asteer!
A noble oun indeed, far-kenn'd an' famed,
Fit for a capital, and Berwick named.

From Aberdeen to Bristol, trace the coast,—
Was there a toun that could owre Berwick
    boast?
Nae toun but ane—ane was the most an' least;
London stude first, and Berwick it cam' neist.

What gallants braw within this toun were seen !
What bouncing lasses blessed thir gallants'
    een !
What merchants grave, what busy 'prentice
    loons,
An' what a thrang o' legs an' din o' soun's !
The kilted fishwife skirlin' cods an' skates,
The stoopit plow-man clatterin' wi' his buits,
The menstrils tootin' different airs at ance,
The bluegoons fechtin' wi' the tykes for banes,
The cuisser's heels upon the causey ringin',
The lame man cursin', an' the blind man singin' ;
While here an' there, like shadows thro' the
    toun,
The sandal'd freers gaed saftly up an' doun,
The black freers an' the grey ; but, frockt in
    white,
Like sunbeam rather show'd the Carmelite.

Of famous convents in this toun were two,
The Great Cross Abbey and the Maison Dew :
Within the Abbey when he list to dwell

Ruled Father John—of whom my tale I tell;
A vigorous Abbot of his age, and fresh,
But little mortified of soul or flesh,
He prowl'd about in secret paths by night,—
His piety was only for the light.
Sleekit he was, an' carefu' to conceal,
And vulnerable only at the heel.

Within that other house, the Manse of God,
Amang the lave twa simple freers abode,
Of little piety, but less pretence,
And not without a cast of common-sense.

Unlike in looks they were, and age, and size,
But mated weel in every other wise;
Easy they were, without one spark of pride;
They lookit on, an' loot the warld slide.

Robert, the taller and the younger freer,
Was a lean brother of a sober cheer;

While Allan, some-deal auld, an' short, an'
    round,
Gaed smiling wi' his een upon the ground.

Their friendship was not feign'd, nor new to
    mak';
I trow they had nae secrets in their crack;
Close had they been, an' constant, mony a year;
Atween the twa ye had a single freer.

Now to my tale: As it befell one day
(Mild was the morning, and the month was May)
Thir twa white freers set aff upon their rounds,
Rejois'd like laddies to evade their bounds.

Their road by Melrose an' by Jethart lay,
A three-weeks wander, an' a weel-kenn'd way, —
For they were chosen every year sans faile
To pass amang the brethren of the dale,
Report of Haly Kirk, and how it stood,
An' lift an antern awmous as they could.

Heartsome it was to hear upon their way
"Ho, Robert!" an' "Hoo, Allan!" owre the
    lay,
Wi' mony a welcome at the landwart toun,
An' mony a saft an' social sitting doun ;—
For weel our freers could dally wi' the wives,
An' tell them tales o' saints' an' sinners' lives ;
Nor less, when at the Abbeys up-o'-land,
Could silent hear, be mute and understand.

At last their Easter holiday was ended,
An' the last day was come as hame they wended.

It was a day o' darkness, wind, an' rain,
Mist on the hills, an' puddles on the plain,
As doun the gate, hungry, an' tired, an' weet,
Toiled Rab and Allan, silent wi' sair feet.

Puir Allan stotted on at half a race,
The smile was deein' on his dismal face ;
Blae were his cheeks that had outbloom'd the
    rose,

And a cauld drap hung ever at his nose.
He hardly lookit as in trim for travel—
Hark i' your lug ! he had a touch o' gravel—
And now an' then he groan'd ; yet all the while
Disown'd his sufferings with a dreary smile.

Robert was weet, an' lank, but het o' blude,
An' strong an' swank, an' carried a hiech head
And in a bundle a' the gear they needed ;
An' grim an' lichtly owre the puddles speeded.

By this, an early gloamin' brocht the nicht
Afore its time, an' Berwick was in sicht,
When Allan spak'—"Robert, I meikle fear
The burgh's yetts are closed ere we win near ;
And we're baith tired and wat, an' fain wad
      hame ;
If herbour's near, I wuss I kenn'd its name."

"There's only Symon Lowrie's," answer'd
      Robert,
" Decent aneuch, if he's at hame an' sober't,—

But, gudesake ! Allan, haud your heart aboun,
An' lift your taes—I'm sure we'll reach the
     toun."

Erelang the road led doun a steep decline ;
They turn'd a bend, an' there was Symon's sign :
A couthie alehouse, by the roadside set,
Ahint a boortree and an open yett,
Wi' the twa cross-keys on a creakin' board,—
The gift to Peter of his gracious Lord.

The reek rase from its hospitable lum,
An' promis'd warmth, at least, to all an' some.
" We'se heat our fingers, an' we'se rest our fit,
An' we'se be better furnish'd ere we flit "—
The words were Allan's, an' the wish was Rab's ;
So in they turn'd their noses an' their gabs.

The house was baith a tavern and a taft,
Land to the front o't, an' the grund was saft—
Na ! mair nor saft ; it was a dounricht mire,
Where ducks micht dabble to their heart's desire.

Into the slough our travellers stoutly ventur'd,
And up the staps, and in the alehouse enter'd,
An' there was Symon's marrow i' the trance
Wha stood and ee'd them wi' nae welcome
    glance.
She was a comely wife—but had the name
Thro' Berwick of "a ding an' dangerous dame."

Allan curcuddied, Robert bow'd an' beckit,
She neither took their reverence, nor rejeckit.

Then brother Robert speer'd for the gudeman—
"How's honest Symmie?" and she answer'd
    than:
"He gaed fra hame," quo' she, "last Waddins-
    day,
To see an' buy a pickle corn an' hay,
And ither things whereof we stand in need."
To which says Robert—"And I wuss him speed!
And may he sune return as sound an' haill
As when he started. But we'll taste your ale;

For tho' I'm weet without as far's the skin,
I maun confess I'm dry aneuch within."

She fill'd the stowp, and brocht oot cheese an'
    bread,
An' doun they sat, and a blythe supper made.

But Allan was a man of social mood,
An' made, where'er he gaed, gude neibourhood,
An' sune he liftit up his voice to cry
"Come hither, dame, an' sit ye doun me by,
An' kiss the caup—richt welcome sall ye be;"
An' blinkit on her wi' a faither's ee.
An' Robert added, as the wife was sweer,
"We'se pay ye well—of that have ye no fear."

An' now twa blythe freers by the blazin' fire
Sat as they settled, and enjoy'd their tire;
An' spake their news to please the dorty dame,
An' drank their swats, an' thocht themsel's at
    hame.

Richt in the middle o' a merry tale
The roll of Berwick drum cam' up the dale ;
An' their ain Abbey bells, borne on the blast,
Rang in their lugs the hour of grace was
    past.
Happy they were ;—but now, without a doot,
The yetts were closed, an' they were lockit
    oot !
Then the gudewife they pray'd, as weel they
    micht,
To grant them herbour for that single nicht.

"What ! herbour freers ? an' the gudeman fra
    hame ?
The Virgin keep the scandal fra my name !
An' what would Symon say, in sic a case,
But in his absence I abus'd his place !
Had I thocht this ye'd never gotten in ;—
And as it is, it's late aneuch for sin ;
Ye maun be stappin'; gang your wa's," says
    she,
And up she gat with danger in her ee.

" Surely ye canna mean the thing ye say,"
Auld Allan said ; " we'd baith be dead ere day
A lang late road ! but even safe suppose't,
It leads to nae gate, for the yetts are clos't.
Ye wouldna hae us, perish'd i' the dark,
Return'd upon your hand at morning stark?
Therefore, for very need, we maun bide still,—
In a' thing else submittin' to your will ;
Little we seek, nor meikle mair desire—
Our boddom-breadths and a sma' blink o'
    fire."

She glanced a troubled look fra freer to freer,
An' spak' at last—" At least ye'se no' be here ;
But gin ye list to lig into the laft,
There's a braw flure-head, an' fatigue mak's
    saft—
Or Meg can look ye up some orra claes :
That, or the road ! mak' up your minds, an'
    chüse ;
And not one further favour need ye speer,
For, on no wise, will I repair have here !"

Wi' that she sent some blankets on before,
Turn'd to her huswifeskep, and no words
more.

Since better couldna be, they were content,
Follow'd the lass, an' to the laft they went ;
A roomy place, abune the hallan wrocht.
Meg made their bed, an' left them to their
thocht,
An' closed the trap, an' took the steps away;
And, lodged at least, sae far they had their
way.

Auld Allan loot a pech, an' laid him doun,
Shot oot his legs, and sune was sleepin'
soun ;
But Rab, tho' tryin' a' the airts at anes,
Fand aye the bed at variance wi' his banes ;
Till, rowin' to the wa', he spied a chink,
An', lookin' doun,—" I'll watch that wife, I
think ;
She's far owre clever for an honest woman ;
But wait a bit—something by ordinar's comin' ! "

He was not wrang; for that same nicht, nae
    less,
She had a supper to devise an' dress,
An' loving company to entertain,
And all that company was only ane.
It was not Symon, on the hunt for strae—
St. Julian be his hap where'er he gae !
It was that rovin' minion of the mirk,
Black John, the Abbot of the Great Cross Kirk!

DUNBAR FLYTING.

Thou speiris, dastard, gif I dar with the fecht.

THY backside bare, thy very inside boss,
    Vile gang-there-oot, that livest but to sorn,
Thou brings the Carrick clay to Embro' cross,
    Hobblin' on buitts that are as hard as horn ;
    Strae-wisps stick oot whaur that the walts are
        worn ;
Come thou again to shame us wi' thy straes
    And we shall scail oor schules, an' put to scorn,
An' stane thee up the causey whaur thou gaes !

Sune as they see thy snout an' lantern jaws
    The bairns cry oot "Here comes oor ain
        queer clark !"
Then flees thou like a howlet chas'd by craws,
    While at thy buit-heels a' the toon tykes
        bark :

Up flee the windows—mutches fra the dark
Peer oot, an' cry " Look, whaur the rascal gaes!
   The gallace-face! I see he wants a sark,
I rede ye, kimmers, tak' in your linen claes ! "

Then rins thou doun the gate, with noise of
        boys,
   And a' the toon tykes hingin' at thy heels;
Of lads an' loons there rises sic a noise,
   Auld aivers tak' the road wi' rattlin' wheels;
   An' cadger-pownies cast baith coals an' creels
For noise o' thee an' clatter o' thy buits;
   Fishwives let drive at thee wi' guts an' squeals
That clash around thy lugs and clod thy cuits!

A WELCOME TO THE LORD TREASURER.

Time—PENSION DAY AT THE MARTINMAS TERM.

I thocht lang quhile sum lord come hame.

I WEARIED lang till ane cam' hame
 Fra whom I fain wad kindness claim;
His name, sae swect, I will declare—
It's you, my ain Lord Treasurér.

Owre every man except the King,
Except the crown owre every thing,
Wi' a' my micht, tho' it was mair,
Welcome, my ain Lord Treasurér!

When I for payment did assay,
Ye promised "Sune—on sic a day;"
And here we are, a punctual pair,—
Welcome, my ain Lord Treasurér!

Ye keep your tryst sae wonder weel,
I haud ye true as Carron steel;
Needs nane your payment to despair—
Welcome, my ain Lord Treasurér!

Nae doot but I'd been singin' dule
To gang without my wage till Yule;
Now I can sing, with heart unsair,
Welcome, my ain Lord Treasurér!

Welcome, my benefice and my rent,
That comes when my last plack is spent;
Welcome, my pension, sure an' fair,—
Welcome, my ain Lord Treasurér!

Welcome, as heartily as I can,
My ain dear maister to your man,
And to your servant evermair—
Welcome, my ain Lord Treasurér!

TO AN EDITOR.

My Prince in God gif the guid grace.

NOO that the time for wussin's near,
  The yokin' o' anither year,—
Sound sleep, an' fingers haill an' fier,
I wuss ye for your hansel here.

Warm be your heart as heretofore,
Your hand as liberal as of yore,
Your basket fu', and a fu' store,
Be yours fra noo till Ninety-four.

As sweetly may ye draw an' drive,
As bauldly may ye rug an' rive,
As stoutly for the Union strive,
And greener yet your Thistle thrive!

Nae hoax nor vile canard come near ye,
Nae fine nor litigation fear ye,
Nae braggin' rival start nor steer ye,
But aye your merits mair endear ye !

Clear be your head, an' quick your ee,
Thrang may your quills an' columns be,
And wider yet your numbers flee—
And that's the New Year wuss o' me.

Quod Hugh Haliburton,
on 31st December 1892.

Glossary.

GLOSSARY.

Aboon, above; in heaven.

Ae, one.

Aforrow, before.

Ain, own.

Aiver, work-horse.

Amáne, amen, end.

Antern, occasional — one here and one there; (literally) "adventuring," or wandering.

Ask Waddinsday, Ash Wednesday.

Aucht, possession; from "owe" = "own."

Awmous, alms—by elision of *l*, peculiar to Scots and French.

Baith, both.

Bairn, child, descendant; from "bear."

Belang'd them = belonged to them.

Bide, endure; abide.

Blink, glimpse, or gleam.

Blue-goons, privileged mendicants who wore the uniform of a blue gown.

Bobbit, danced.

Boddom, bottom.

Bools, balls. From Fr. "boule."

Boortree, elder-tree, *not* alder; planted at gates and in gardens to keep away imps; called also "boontree" and "boo'try."

8

Boss, empty, hollow.

Bowff, to bow or bark ; an imitative word.

Braird, the first appearance of the leaf of germinating corn; what Chaucer calls "the tendre croppes."

Bude, behoved—with the idea of obligation or necessity.

Buits, phonetically for "boots."

Burn, a brook. To fling anything down the burn is to part with it for ever.

Cadger, travelling-merchant.

Ca's, calls ; drives.

Cast, the quantity thrown to one's lot.

Can'les, candles.

Cantit, leaning to one side; or on the edge.

Carline, an old wife; from "ceorl." "Carle" is an old man.

'Chacker, Exchequer.

Chappin, a quart.

Chaumer, chamber.

Cheeny, china.

Chiel',
Chield, } young man, or lad.

Chucky-stane, a small quartz pebble; named from the sound.

Chüse, choose.

Claes, clothes.

Cleed, clothe.

Clegs or *Glegs*, gadflies, or " goad "-flies.

Clock, hatch—said of a brood-hen; from the sound.

Cockerty, unsteadily poised.

Cuisser, courser.

Covetice, covetousness, greed.

Couthie, comfortable or home-like, because known; from "cunnan," to know.

Crack, cannon; from the sound.

Crap, harvest; also craw, or stomach. Crop.

Crenns, herons, cranes.

Crony, chum. From "crone," an old woman, or gossip.

Cuist, cast.

Cuits, ankles.

Cummer, gossip: French, "com-mère." Also "kimmer."

Curcuddy, to curtsey low; a child's game.

Dally, to gossip leisurely. Chaucer's Friar also knew "moche of daliaunce."

Dangerous, imperious, dictatorial. Antonio lay within Shylock's "danger"—*i.e.*, his power.

Dew, Fr. Dieu.

Ding, for "digne," dignified, or haughty.

'Dite, compose; write. From Lat. "dictum."

Disport, comfort and pleasure.

Doucely, agreeably: Fr. "doux."

Dourness, obstinacy: Fr. "dur."

Dovering, dozing.

Drie, endure.

Drumlie, turbid.

Dune, done.

Dyke, a wall; (originally) a bank thrown up by "digging." A dike in England is a trench.

Ear', early.

Ee, eye.

Fain, fond, delighted; "fœgen"=glad.

Fa'in', falling.

Fash, to trouble.

Fasherie, trouble.

Fashious, troublesome; from Fr. "fâcher," to bother.

Fauld, fold, enclosure, garden.

Fause, false: Fr. "faux."

'Fend, defend.

Flingin'-tree, flail.

Flure-head, floor-top or area.

Flyting, scolding.

Fool, fowl.

Fore-nenst, over-against.

Forfoughen, exhausted with toil; "for" is intensive.

Forrat, forward.

Gade, went.

Gallace, gallows.

Gang, walk.

Gang-there-oot, vagrant.

Gar, make, compel.

Gawin', galling: "galler," Old French.

Gear, property.

Gey, pretty; "gey weel" = "pretty well."

Gif or *Gin*, if.

Glower, look staringly.

Gowff, golf. "Kolf," Dutch for a club.

Greet, weep; "gretan."

Haill, whole.

Hallan', hall-end; wall of public room, screening the doorway.

Hantle, a good quantity.

Haud, hold.

Hear'stane, hearth-stone.

Hed, had.

Hiech, high.

Hinged brigs, drawbridges.

Hoast, cough.

Hochs, hocks or the back of the knee-joints.

Howff, place of familiar resort; haven.

Howp, hope.

Huswifeskep, housewifeship; household affairs.

Ilka, each.

I'se, I shall.

Ither, other.

Jethart, Jedburgh.

Jinkin', dodging, slipping.

John, Joan.

Kenna, know not.

Kepit, protected.

Kintra, country.

Laft, loft.
Laidly, loathsome.
Lauch, laugh.
Lave, left, the rest.
Lay, lea.
Leal, loyal.
Lest, last, endure.
Lig, lie; "licgan."
Limmer, a dissolute female.
Lintie, linnet.
Loot, let, let escape.
Lo'esome, lovely.
Loup, leap.
Lout, stoop; from "lútan."
Lowsed, loosed.
Lug, ear.
Lum, chimney (corner).

Maen, moan, to lament (for).
Maist, most.
Mak', make, compose; *cp.* "poiein," Greek.
Makar, poet.
Marrow, mate; from "marry."
Mell, meddle, mix; from "mesler," Old Fr.

Mense, discretion.
Mirk, murk, darkness.
Mull, mule.
Mutch, a woman's white cap.
Mutchkin, a pint.

Nar'd, near it.
Naysay, denial.
Near-be-gaun, illiberal.
Nether = an adder; "næ-dre," a snake.
Nice, careful of trifles.
Nippit, parsimonious.

O'ercome, surplus.
Orra, extra.
Owre, over.
Pech, groan, sigh.
Pend, hung roof or archway; "pendre," French.
Pens, feathers, wings.
Plack, a small coin, $\frac{1}{3}$d. Scots!
Popinjay, parrot; (literally) a chattering cock,—which is also the literal meaning of "babbly-jock."

Quean, young woman; "cwen."

Rane, murmur monotonously; "rún," a whisper. "Roun," or "round" in Middle English.

Rede, counsel; "ræd," advice.

Rent, income. Fr. "rente"; from "reddere," Lat.

Rins, runs.

Rookit, left destitute.

Roums, landed property, or income therefrom.

Sair, sore.

Sark, shirt.

Scaith, scathe, injury; "scatha."

Scart, scratch; a miser.

Scaur'd, scared, frightened.

'Sey, essay, try.

Shae, shoe.

Shaw, show; plantation.

Sichin, sighing.

Siller, silver; money.

Skail, scatter, spill.

Skirlin', screeching.

Sleekit, plump and glossy.

Snap (o' cauld), blizzard.

Some-deal, somewhat.

Sorn, live meanly at another's expense.

Soums, sums (of money).

Sowpin', imbibing, sipping; "súpan."

Souple, supple.

Speir, ask.

Stangs, stings.

Stank, fosse; stagnating water in a ditch.

Stechy, stiff and heavy.

Steekit, shut.

St. Julian, the patron-saint of travellers; hospitality.

Stock and rent, property and income.

Stoiter, stagger.

Stoopit, stooped, bent.

Stotted, stumbled; bounded and rolled.

Stour, dust; battle.

Spulzie, spoil, plunder.

Swank, tall and agile.

Swick, cheat. "Swic," deceit.

Swink, toil; "swincan."

Swith, quickly, immediately; " swithé."

Syne, ago ; then.

Tack, lease, possession.

Tae, toe.

Taft, messuage, farmhouse.

Tass, cup.

Thereanent, about or with it.

Thir, these ; *Thae,* those.

Tholin', tolerating, bearing.

Thoums, thumbs.

Thrang, company.

Thrawart, contrary.

Tint, lost; *tyne,* lose.

Toun, farmstead; town.

Towbooth or *tolbooth,* jail.

Towls, toils.

Trance, passage: Lat. " trans."

Tryst, engagement.

Trap, ladder; hatch. "Trappa," a stair, is the Swedish original.

Tumed or *toomed,* emptied.

Tyke, dog.

Unquit, unrequited.

Wair'd, spent.

Wale, select.

Wan, won.

Wander, pilgrimage.

War, were.

Warrand, warrant; "garantir," Old French.

Wa's, ways; walls.

Wat, wit, know: "witan."

Wauk, waken; lie awake; "wacian."

Weebie, ragwort.

Weirs, wars.

Whaup, curlew; imitative.

Whummle, fall heavily by overbalancing; tumble heels o'er head.

Wir, our; from "we."   *Wuss*, wish.
Wite, blame; "wite,"
      punishment.   *Yarrow*, milfoil; in German,
Wad, mad; eager. "Wod"   " garbe."
      = mad in Old Eng-   *Yett*, gate.
      lish.   *Yule*, Christmastide.

NOTE.—The English reader will please to observe that words which are not eye- may yet be perfect ear-rhymes in the Scottish language; thus (*v.* p. 31) the words "fear," "puir," "gear," and "sure" are perfect rhymes, to be pronounced like the French "fleur."

THE WALTER SCOTT PRESS, NEWCASTLE-ON-TYNE.

SCOTTISH POETS

ISSUED IN THE CANTERBURY POETS SERIES.

Each in Two Volumes, Cloth, Cut or Uncut, 1s. per Volume.

POEMS AND SONGS OF ROBERT BURNS. With a Prefatory Notice, Biographical and Critical, by JOSEPH SKIPSEY.

POEMS OF SIR WALTER SCOTT. With Prefatory Notice, Biographical and Critical, by WILLIAM SHARP.

Each in one Volume, Cloth, Cut or Uncut, 1s.

POEMS BY ALLAN RAMSAY. Selected and arranged, with a Biographical Sketch of the Poet, by J. LOGIE ROBERTSON.

POEMS OF JAMES HOGG, THE ETTRICK SHEP-HERD. With Introduction by Mrs. GARDEN.

POEMS OF THOMAS CAMPBELL. With Prefatory Notice, Biographical and Critical, by JOHN HOGBEN.

JACOBITE SONGS AND BALLADS [Selected]. Edited, with Notes and Introductory Note, by G. S. MACQUOID.

BORDER BALLADS. Edited, with Introduction and Notes, by GRAHAM R. TOMSON.

POEMS OF OSSIAN. With an Introduction, Historical and Critical, by GEORGE EYRE-TODD.

POEMS OF THE SCOTTISH MINOR POETS, from the Age of Ramsay to David Gray. Selected and Edited by Sir G. DOUGLAS, Bart.

CONTEMPORARY SCOTTISH VERSE (including Selections from William Bell Scott, Professor Blackie, Lord Southesk, Hugh Haliburton, R. L. Stevenson, Andrew Lang, George MacDonald, John Davidson, etc.). Edited by Sir GEORGE DOUGLAS, Bart.

May also be had in the following Bindings:—Red Roan, gilt edges, 2s. 6d.; Padded Morocco, gilt edges, 5s.; Padded Calf, 6s.; and in Half-Morocco, gilt top, antique.

Also in SPECIAL CLOTH BINDING, with **Photogravure Frontispiece**, 2s. per Vol.

London: WALTER SCOTT, LIMITED, Paternoster Square.

Square 8vo, Cloth, Price 2s. 6d.

LAYS OF THE
HIGHLANDS AND ISLANDS

By JOHN STUART BLACKIE,

Emeritus Professor of Greek in the University of Edinburgh.

———

"Visitors to the Hebrides and the Highlands would not do amiss to make a companion of Professor Blackie's *Lays of the Highlands and Islands* (Walter Scott), if only for the stirring and characteristic 'Talk with the Tourists' which forms the preface. This introductory address is scarcely less fervid in tone than the picturesque ballads—such as the 'Death of Columba'—or the various 'poems of places.' These last are arranged under the names of the counties in which the localities that inspire the poet are to be found, so that the traveller may read under the beneficent influence of the *genus loci.*"—*Saturday Review.*

———

London: WALTER SCOTT, LIMITED, Paternoster Square.

Crown 8vo, Cloth Elegant, Price 3s. 6d. With several Full-page Illustrations.

THE NEW BORDER TALES.

By Sir GEORGE DOUGLAS, Bart.

"The tales are all written in a fine romantic spirit, and have on them the impress of the genius of the places whence they come. They make a delightful volume, scarcely less pleasing by reason of its own merits than by the old associations which it reawakens."—*Scotsman.*

"Told in a brief, straightforward fashion, and in somewhat old-fashioned language, they call up the glamour, the romance, and the lonesomeness of the Border country. They tell of ghosts and ghostly memories, of dark pages from family histories, of hidden treasure, of strange madness, and strong passions."—*The Bookman.*

London : WALTER SCOTT. LIMITED, Paternoster Square.

BOOKS OF FAIRY TALES.

Crown 8vo, Cloth Elegant, Price 3s. 6d. per vol.

ENGLISH FAIRY AND OTHER FOLK TALES.

Selected and Edited, with an Introduction,
By EDWIN SIDNEY HARTLAND.

With 12 Full-Page Illustrations by CHARLES E. BROCK.

SCOTTISH FAIRY AND FOLK TALES.

Selected and Edited, with an Introduction,
By SIR GEORGE DOUGLAS, BART.

With 12 Full-Page Illustrations by JAMES TORRANCE.

IRISH FAIRY AND FOLK TALES.

Selected and Edited, with an Introduction,
By W. B. YEATS.

With 12 Full-Page Illustrations by JAMES TORRANCE.

London : WALTER SCOTT, LIMITED, Paternoster Square.

*Quarto, cloth elegant, gilt edges, emblematic design on
.cover, 6s. May also be had in a variety
of Fancy Bindings.*

THE

MUSIC OF THE POETS:

A MUSICIANS' BIRTHDAY BOOK.

EDITED BY ELEONORE D'ESTERRE KEELING.

THIS is a unique Birthday Book. Against each date are
given the names of musicians whose birthday it is, together
with a verse-quotation appropriate to the character of their
different compositions or performances. A special feature of
the book consists in the reproduction in fac-simile of autographs, and autographic music, of living composers. Three
sonnets by Mr. Theodore Watts, on the "Fausts" of Berlioz,
Schumann, and Gounod, have been written specially for this
volume. It is illustrated with designs of various musical
instruments, etc.; autographs of Rubenstein, Dvoràk, Greig,
Mackenzie, Villiers Stanford, etc., etc.

London : WALTER SCOTT, LIMITED, Paternoster Square.

SPECIAL THREE-VOLUME SETS.

BY OLIVER WENDELL HOLMES—

SET No. 1. { THE AUTOCRAT OF THE BREAKFAST-TABLE. THE POET AT THE BREAKFAST-TABLE. THE PROFESSOR AT THE BREAKFAST-TABLE.

BY WALTER SAVAGE LANDOR—

SET No. 2. { IMAGINARY CONVERSATIONS. THE PENTAMERON. PERICLES AND ASPASIA.

THREE ENGLISH ESSAYISTS—

SET No. 3. { ESSAYS OF ELIA (CHARLES LAMB). ESSAYS OF LEIGH HUNT. ESSAYS OF WILLIAM HAZLITT.

THREE CLASSICAL MORALISTS—

SET No. 4. { THE MORALS OF SENECA. THE TEACHINGS OF EPICTETUS. THE MEDITATIONS OF MARCUS AURELIUS.

BY HENRY DAVID THOREAU—

SET No. 5. { WALDEN. A WEEK ON THE CONCORD AND MERRIMAC RIVERS. MISCELLANEOUS ESSAYS.

FAMOUS LETTERS—

SET No. 6. { LETTERS OF BYRON. LETTERS OF SHELLEY. LETTERS OF BURNS.

LOWELL SERIES—

SET No. 7 { MY STUDY WINDOWS. THE ENGLISH POETS. THE BIGLOW PAPERS.

Three Vols., Crown 8vo, Cloth, Gilt Top, in Shell Case, Price 4/6.
Three Vols., Crown 8vo, Cloth, Gilt Top, in Cloth Pedestal Case, 5s.

May also be had separately at 1s. 6d. each.

Also in Half Morocco, Gilt Top; and full Roan, Gilt Edges,
Shell Case.

London: WALTER SCOTT, LIMITED, Paternoster Square.

www.ingramcontent.com/pod-product-compliance
Lightning Source LLC
Chambersburg PA
CBHW032012010726
47493CB00007B/2372